LIGHTNING STRIKES TWICE

ESCAPING GREAT EXPECTATIONS

BY Jan Fields

Published by Magic Wagon, a division of the ABDO Group, PO Box 398166, Minneapolis, MN 55439. Copyright © 2013 by Abdo Consulting Group, Inc. International copyrights reserved in all countries. All rights reserved. No part of this book may be reproduced in any form without written permission from the publisher.

Calico Chapter Books™ is a trademark and logo of Magic Wagon.

Printed in the United States of America, North Mankato, Minnesota.
102012
012013
 This book contains at least 10% recycled materials.

Written by Jan Fields
Cover illustration by Scott Altmann
Edited by Stephanie Hedlund and Grace Hansen
Cover and interior design by Neil Klinepier

Library of Congress Cataloging-in-Publication Data
Fields, Jan.
  Lightning strikes twice : escaping Great expectations / by Jan Fields ; [illustrator, Scott Altmann].
    p. cm. -- (Adventures in extreme reading ; bk. 4)
  Summary: Uncle Dan is back, and with him is the beautiful Tempest St. Cloud with a promise of unlimited funding--but Carter's cousin Isabelle is suspicious, and when a demonstration excursion into Great expectations results in zombies and murderers Carter does not know what to think.
  ISBN 978-1-61641-922-6
1. Dickens, Charles, 1812-1870. Great expectations--Juvenile fiction. 2. Virtual reality--Juvenile fiction. 3. Computer hackers--Juvenile fiction. 4. Books and reading--Juvenile fiction. 5. Inventions--Juvenile fiction. 6. Cousins--Juvenile fiction. 7. Uncles--Juvenile fiction. [1. Dickens, Charles, 1812-1870. Great expectations--Fiction. 2. Virtual reality--Fiction. 3. Computer hackers--Fiction. 4. Books and reading--Fiction. 5. Inventions--Fiction. 6. Cousins--Fiction. 7. Uncles--Fiction.] I. Altmann, Scott, ill. II. Title.
  PZ7.F479177Lig 2013
  813.6--dc23   2012028636

Table of Contents

MOONIE

Carter Lewis jumped when he felt a light smack on the back of his head. He looked up from his book and into the grinning face of his best friend, Matt.

"Are you actually reading?" Matt asked. He looked in surprise at the thick book in Carter's hand. Then his eyes widened. "I didn't miss an English assignment, did I?"

"No, I just felt like reading," Carter said.

"You must have a fever." Matt reached out to put a hand on Carter's forehead. Carter swatted it away.

"Did you want something, for real?" Carter asked.

Matt slid into the chair across from Carter at the lunchroom table. "Dad bought me Cow Racer 2 over the weekend, because my report

4

card was decent." Then his eyes widened. "Oh, man, is that why you're reading a fifty-pound book? Did you get busted for your report card?"

"No, my report card was fine. This is a good book." Carter leaned back in his chair, stretching his long legs out to crowd Matt on the other side of the table.

Matt leaned forward and pulled on the book so he could see the cover. "*Frankenstein*? Wasn't that a really old movie?"

"The book's different."

Matt shrugged. "Hey, it's your brain cells. So, do you want to come over and race cows?"

"Sure," Carter said.

The bell rang for the end of the lunch period. Carter shoved a bookmark in his book and dropped it in his backpack with a thump. Matt was right about one thing, the book weighed a ton.

Carter hadn't lied about the book—not really. It was good, but that's not why he was reading it. He was reading it because of his uncle Dan.

Uncle Dan was a crazy smart computer programmer and inventor. He'd invented the coolest virtual reality tech. Most virtual reality gear involved a helmet or goggles with speakers to let you see and hear the virtual reality world. Uncle Dan's VR suit let you smell it, taste it, and feel it, too. And every one of Uncle Dan's virtual reality worlds came from a classic book.

The only problem was that some crazy hacker had tried to ruin the program. Carter had ended up battling the hacker in the virtual world more than once. After the last time, Carter had realized something. It was a lot easier to win the war if you'd already read the book.

So he'd gotten into classic books.

On the up side, his report card really rocked. On the down side, his backpack weighed a ton. And his friends were starting to notice. Carter didn't want anyone expecting him to be some super smart nerd type. They already had one kid in the family for that job. He just wanted to know enough to help his uncle.

"Carter!"

Speak of the nerd, Carter thought as he turned to face Isabelle. "I'm on my way to algebra," he yelled.

"I know," Isabelle said.

Carter rolled his eyes. Of course, she knew everything. "What exactly do you need, Izzy?"

"Has Uncle Dan talked to you lately?" she asked.

Carter shook his head. "I've barely seen him since he got back."

"Well," she said, "Storm did pretend to kidnap him just a couple weeks ago. I think we should check up on him."

"You mean go over there?" Carter asked. Uncle Dan tended to be a little paranoid and he didn't like uninvited drop-ins. Just showing up didn't seem like a good idea at all.

Isabelle sighed and shoved a strand of limp, blonde hair behind her ear. "He might not like it," she said, "but I think he needs to be checked up on once in a while."

"So why not call him?"

She frowned for a moment. "He isn't taking my calls."

"He's not answering his phone?" Carter felt a flush of worry. Uncle Dan always answered his phone.

"Not exactly." Isabelle pulled Carter out of the main hall and into a small alcove. She took out her cell phone and punched in Uncle Dan's number. Using a cell phone in the school was strictly against the rules. Since Isabelle was normally the queen of rules, Carter knew she must be worried about their uncle.

She put her phone up to Carter's ear so he could listen to his uncle's voicemail message. "If you're hearing this message, I'm either away from the phone or this is Isabelle. If I'm away from the phone, leave a quick message and I'll get back to you. If this is Isabelle, hang up. I'll call you when I need you."

Carter raised an eyebrow. "Just how many times have you called him?"

8

"A few," she said.

"Sounds like a lot."

Isabelle huffed. "I don't like being shut out. We worked hard to get this project working for Uncle Dan. Why is he shutting us out now? I don't like it."

"Maybe he just doesn't need us right now."

"And maybe Storm is torturing him for information right this second."

Carter stared at his cousin. "You have a much scarier imagination than I thought. Look, I've got to get to class."

Isabelle stepped in front of him and put her hands on her hips. "Promise you'll go over there with me this afternoon."

"Isabelle, he doesn't want to be bothered."

"Promise," she said. "Or . . . or . . . I'll tell everyone that you wet the bed when you were ten."

"Hey!" Carter snapped. "I had a fever and Mom was loading me with liquids. That's just rotten."

"So is leaving Uncle Dan in the clutches of that hacker," Isabelle said.

"Okay, I'll come with you—as long as you leave me alone now."

"You got it." She smirked as she spun on her heel and jogged off to her own class. Not that a teacher would mind if Isabelle was late. They would assume some horrible, unavoidable accident must have happened. Not like Carter. He groaned, hiked his book bag up on his shoulder, and headed for algebra.

Mr. Jarvis gave Carter the stink eye as he eased open the classroom door and slipped in. Luckily, the algebra teacher was in the middle of explaining some formula and didn't want to interrupt his flow to yell.

Carter hauled his algebra book out of his book bag and looked over at Jina's desk to see what page they were on. She smiled at him and scooted her book a little closer so he could see.

"Mr. Lewis," the algebra teacher called from the front, "since you've finally graced us with your presence, perhaps you could share your brilliance as well. Come up and work number twelve on the board for us."

Carter looked down at the page and groaned softly. Sometimes he hated his cousin.

The rest of the school day went about as well as algebra class. When he got to gym class, he remembered he'd torn the seat out of his gym shorts and had to borrow a spare pair from the lost and found. The new shorts were too big and Carter was pretty sure he mooned the class at least twice.

Then when they headed for the shower, Matt erased all doubt by calling him "Moonie" as he walked by. The showers were cold enough to set his teeth chattering. When he finally pulled on his street clothes as fast as possible, he was ready to just put the school day behind him.

"Are you going to get off the bus at my house or come over later?" Matt asked.

Carter groaned again. "I'm sorry, Matt. I forgot. I have to go with Isabelle to Uncle Dan's house. I don't think we're going to be there very long, but I'm not sure. I'll come over after that if I can."

"You hang out with your cousin too much," Matt said, shaking his head. "I tell you, dude, it's not natural."

Carter nodded. "Tell me about it."

As they walked to the bus, Carter wondered if Isabelle was just feeling left out of Uncle Dan's work. They'd worked hard to help their uncle, and he could see how Isabelle might feel pushed out. Still, what if she was right? What if something had happened to Uncle Dan?

As soon as Carter dumped his backpack inside the front door, he yelled, "I'm home!"

His mom poked her head around the corner. "Hi," she said. "Do you have any homework? If so, grab a snack and get on it. You want to keep those grades up while you're on a roll."

Carter shook his head. "Nothing tonight. Isabelle wants to meet me at Uncle Dan's house. I'll grab a snack over there."

His mom beamed. His parents loved it when he spent time with Isabelle. He suspected they hoped her brainiac ways were rubbing off on him.

"Okay, sweetie. Don't be late for supper."

"I won't." He turned and trotted out to get his bike. At least meeting up with Isabelle had saved him the grilling he would have gotten if he'd asked to go to Matt's house to play his new game.

When he reached Uncle Dan's house, Carter spotted a car he didn't recognize in the driveway. Uncle Dan never left his electric car in the driveway. He liked all his stuff inside and away from prying eyes. Uncle Dan definitely ranked pretty high on the paranoia scale.

Carter coasted around and dropped his bike behind the trash corral. He saw Isabelle's bike leaning against one of the trash cans. Maybe she'd already found out that Uncle Dan was alive and well. Then Carter could head straight over to Matt's house. He grinned hopefully as he walked up the sidewalk and rang the bell.

The door opened to Uncle Dan's smiling face. "Carter," he said, "this is fantastic. You're just in time. Come on in."

Carter was tempted to ask Uncle Dan for some identification. His uncle was never this cheery. "Have you been napping beside any space pods lately, Uncle Dan?"

Uncle Dan just laughed and pulled Carter inside. Carter looked up from the doorway to the main floor landing. He spotted Isabelle with her arms crossed, looking furious. Beside her was the most gorgeous woman Carter had ever seen.

A Tempest Arrives

"Carter, I want you to meet someone," Uncle Dan said as he half dragged his nephew up the stairs to the landing. "This is Miss Tempest St. Cloud. She represents a group that may invest in my project."

Carter nodded at the smiling woman. "Nice to meet you," he said.

"And you," the woman responded. Now that Carter was on the same landing with her, he saw the woman was about his height—making her taller than Izzy but shorter than Uncle Dan. She had long, dark hair and dark blue eyes. Even in crisp jeans and a silky white shirt, she managed to look dressed up.

"I didn't know you were looking for investors," Carter said, tearing his gaze away from the stranger and looking at Uncle Dan.

"Neither did I," Isabelle added. She still had her arms folded as she glared at the elegant woman beside her.

"I wasn't," Uncle Dan said. "I met Tempest while I was . . . away. We have a lot in common, so I told her a little bit about my project. And then she showed up on my doorstep with an offer from her investment group."

"How nice," Isabelle said. Her voice made it clear that she thought it anything but nice.

Carter didn't say anything, but he did think the timing sounded a little off. Uncle Dan never told anyone about his business. What was so special about this woman? He looked back at his uncle, who was staring at the stranger with big, puppy eyes.

Uncle Dan dragged his eyes away from his guest and rubbed his hands together. "So I was going to give Tempest a demonstration of the prototype. That's why it's so great that you're both here. No one knows the system from inside the suit better than you, Carter. You can suit up and walk her through the experience."

"Today?" he yelped. "Right now?"

"No time like the present," Miss St. Cloud said smoothly.

"Are you sure that's a good idea?" Isabelle asked. "Considering how badly your system was breached recently. Are you sure the programs are safe?"

Carter saw his uncle's face redden.

"Oh dear, Daniel," Miss St. Cloud said, "I had no idea you had security problems. I certainly wouldn't want to be sealed up inside one of your suits if we're not sure they're safe."

"They're perfectly safe," Uncle Dan said, throwing a scowl at Isabelle. "I've isolated the system physically now. I'm not counting on firewalls anymore. The system for the virtual reality is now completely independent of everything. There simply is no way for an outside agency to interfere. They'd have to be right here in this house to do it."

"What if there was bad code left from all the mess that hacker made?" Isabelle asked.

Miss St. Cloud turned toward Uncle Dan again.

"I've gone through everything more than once," he said. "The system is clean. It's completely isolated. You're as safe in the suits as you are right here, right now in the real world."

Miss St. Cloud smiled. "Well, that's certainly good enough for me. Though I would like to hear more about this hacker. How bad was this attack?"

"The hacker messed with several of the books," Isabelle said. "It nearly killed Carter."

"Now, there's no point blowing that story up," Uncle Dan grumbled.

"I don't know," Carter said. "That March Hare with the razor sharp steel teeth did seem to be pretty hostile."

"Oh my," the woman said. "That must have been terrifying. I'm amazed you're willing to go back inside the suits. You must be very brave."

Carter felt his face grow hot from the compliments.

"Yeah, he's a regular superhero," Izzy said.

"Carter handled it very well," Uncle Dan said. "But it was just a program. He was in no real danger."

Carter thought about how the suits were designed to give you the same sensations that happened in the story. When they'd gone into the very first book, *The Three Musketeers*, d'Artagnan had jabbed him with the sword. It hurt a lot and Carter went home bruised. He wasn't sure he would bet on the suits not being able to mash all the air out of him or break a bone.

"I'm glad we never found out exactly how much the suits can hurt you," Carter said.

Uncle Dan gave him another glare. Clearly he didn't want them ruining his chances with the investor, but Carter wasn't sure there was any real benefit in lying to her either.

"So what books have you been in?" Miss St.

Cloud asked.

"We went in *The Three Musketeers* first," Carter said.

"That's when the suit tried to stab him," Izzy threw in.

"Then *Alice in Wonderland*," Carter went on, ignoring his cousin.

"The book tried to chew him up and cut his head off," Izzy said. "Plus a griffin carried me off. It was a long way to the ground if it had dropped me."

"It wouldn't have dropped you," Uncle Dan grumbled.

"Then we went into 'The Legend of Sleepy Hollow,'" Carter said. "That one was really cool. And it didn't exactly try to kill us."

"If you don't count trapping us in the suits until we starved or died of dehydration," Izzy added.

"You guys just had to find the back door," Uncle Dan insisted. "That wasn't even the hacker, just a little mistake on my part." He looked up at Miss St. Cloud and quickly added, "Which I have fixed since then."

"And finally, we were in *Treasure Island*," Carter said. "No one tried really hard to kill me in that one, but the hacker was in it, too. So that was interesting."

"You've been in a program with the person who hacked the system?" Miss St. Cloud asked. Her eyebrows rose so high, they vanished into her bangs.

"We were trying to save Uncle Dan," Izzy said. "From a kidnapper."

"I wasn't kidnapped!" Uncle Dan snapped.

"We didn't know that," Izzy said.

"But we beat the hacker in that one," Carter said. "Actually we've beaten the hacker every time he's tried anything. So you probably wouldn't have to worry."

"Probably?" she asked.

"Definitely," Uncle Dan said firmly. "As I said, my setup downstairs is now physically removed from all other computer networks.

It's impossible for the hacker to get back into the system unless I open the front door and let him in."

"Well, that sounds safe," Miss St. Cloud said with a smile. "Though I'm glad you shared with me the challenges you've all been through. That just makes the end result all the more impressive. So, shall we go and try out the system? I know I'm looking forward to it."

"Right this way," Uncle Dan said as he turned and hurried down the steps. His computer lab was in the basement of the split-level ranch. Isabelle grabbed Carter's arm as he started after his uncle and Miss St. Cloud.

"I don't trust her," Izzy hissed.

Carter watched the slender woman turn and follow his uncle. In all honesty, he didn't really trust her either. She was too quick with the compliments and something about her just felt wrong. And there was something funny with her name.

"There's not much we can do about it," Carter

said. "Uncle Dan seems to think she's okay."

"Uncle Dan isn't thinking clearly," Izzy said.

Carter couldn't argue with that either. Finally he shrugged. "Still doesn't seem like there's much we can do about it."

"We can keep an eye on her," Isabelle said. "And you better be careful. You're the one going in the suit with her."

Carter nodded. He wasn't happy about that either. Still, he had to admit, he wouldn't want to miss another adventure.

"You guys coming?" Uncle Dan's voice carried up the stairs.

"Coming!" Carter yelled, then turned to Isabelle. "So we'll be careful." Then he grinned. "If it's a trap, it won't be the first one we've gotten out of."

"Let's hope those aren't famous last words," Isabelle said.

Then the cousins hurried down the stairs to see exactly what might be waiting for them.

A FRIGHTENING GLITCH

As Carter walked through the door to his uncle's computer lab, he smiled. The room was chaos. Papers, soda cans, and open notebooks covered every bit of space not already taken up with computers, monitors, and other confusing bits and pieces of technology.

When Uncle Dan was away chasing the hacker, Isabelle had cleaned the basement rooms and organized everything to the point of obsession. Somehow seeing it all back to the chaos Uncle Dan preferred made it seem like life was finally getting back to normal.

Carter paid little attention as Uncle Dan explained the computer power necessary to run the virtual reality program. It sounded like a lot to him, but he was really more into using computers than thinking about how they work. He shifted from foot to foot, eager to get on to the part where he climbed into the suit.

He noticed Isabelle didn't seem to share his hurry. She watched their visitor sharply as if expecting her to try to run off with one of the laptops at any moment.

"So a special system will need to be installed in any store that offers patrons a chance to play inside a book," Miss St. Cloud said.

"That's right," Uncle Dan answered. "But that's best anyway. You want the virtual reality on its own system so it isn't influenced by other computer use in the store."

"And how many books will the system come with?" she asked.

"The store will choose what it wants and how many. Right now I'm working only with classics, but eventually I believe we'll be able to afford to use new best sellers. Imagine the sales boost to a book if your reader gets to play in it."

Miss St. Cloud nodded, her eyes wandering over the computers. "And you say these are all totally independent of any outside influence."

"Totally." Uncle Dan was bouncing slightly on his toes, a sure sign he was getting impatient. He wanted to get the demonstration started, but Miss St. Cloud kept poking around the computers and looking them over.

Finally, Uncle Dan walked away from her and threw open the door to the suit room. Isabelle and Carter followed him, peeking into the room to see if their uncle had done anything new with the suits. They looked just the same as always, like giant astronaut puppets hanging from wire and cable "strings" from the ceiling. The suits would have been right at home on the space station.

"These are really the most exciting part of the system," Uncle Dan said, his eyes on the suits. "These suits allow full sensory experience inside them."

Miss St. Cloud made a vague sound, still bent

over one of Uncle Dan's computers. He cleared his throat. Finally, she looked up and smiled.

"You certainly have a nice setup," she said.

"You haven't seen anything yet!"

Miss St. Cloud followed them into the suit room. "Do these suits have limits on how big or small the user can be?"

"Only very reasonable ones," Uncle Dan replied. "You couldn't put a toddler in one or someone unable to walk. But the suits can conform to fit a ten year old or an NBA player."

She nodded, walking around the closest suit. "Very impressive."

"All you have to do is choose which book to explore," Uncle Dan said. "If you don't have a preference, I can pick one."

She smiled and asked, "Do you have *Great Expectations*? I've always loved Charles Dickens."

Carter felt a surge of disappointment. With all the books he'd crammed in his head in the last months, he hadn't read that one.

If she had to pick Dickens, why didn't she pick

A Christmas Carol, he thought glumly. *I've read that one.* Then he thought about the ghosts and shivered.

"Does *Great Expectations* have ghosts?" he asked.

"Not exactly," the slender woman answered. "Though the characters are a bit haunted."

That didn't make much sense to Carter, but he shrugged and said, "Sounds okay to me."

"It starts in a cemetery," Isabelle said slyly.

"Oh, you know the book?" Miss St. Cloud's eyebrows went up in surprise.

"I know most of the books in the program," Isabelle said. "I cleaned out most of the bad code from the hack attack."

Miss St. Cloud looked skeptically at Uncle Dan. "You trusted a child to fix the problems created by a professional hacker?"

Carter saw his cousin's cheeks grow red. He hoped she wasn't going to yell.

"Isabelle is a very competent programmer," Uncle Dan said. Isabelle looked a little calmer until he added, "And I went over all the code again myself, of course."

"You did?" Isabelle snapped, clearly insulted.

"Double checking is just good security," her uncle told her firmly. By the look on his uncle's face, Carter suspected Isabelle was pushing her luck. If she kept going, Uncle Dan was going to send her home.

"Can we suit up?" Carter asked, hoping to distract them from fighting.

"That sounds good," Miss St. Cloud said. "Do we need to wait for you to start the program first?"

"No," Uncle Dan said. He helped his guest into the closest suit and left Isabelle to seal Carter into his. This was the part of the process Carter hated most, standing inside the dark, closed suit. The darkness sealed around him completely and no sound could penetrate the suit. Carter could hear his own heartbeat and his slightly ragged breathing, and that was all.

"Are you both ready?" Uncle Dan's voice

asked in Carter's ear.

"I am," he answered.

"I'm ready," Miss St. Cloud's voice said softly in his other ear.

Often the programs started with a blinding light as they jumped into broad daylight. This time, the darkness remained, softened only by the light of the moon and a scattering of stars. He looked around and could see the rounded shape of tombstones and weeds.

"How amazing."

Carter turned and saw Miss St. Cloud. She wore a long, heavy dress and a bonnet. The hem of the dress dragged on the weedy ground. Carter was glad he wasn't a girl. The graveyard was spooky enough without wearing something you couldn't possibly run in.

"This is fun," Carter muttered. "Starting in a graveyard."

"We need to find Pip," she said.

"Pip?" Carter echoed. That sounded like the name of a dog or a monkey. Just as he spoke, they heard the sound of stumbling feet in the darkness. A kid came out of the shadows. His face was as pale as the moon. He stumbled over roots and knocked into the headstones as he rushed through the graveyard in the dark.

"Pip?" Miss St. Cloud said.

The boy ignored her and pushed between them. He never even looked at them as he rushed back into the darkness.

"What's wrong with him?" Carter asked.

"He must have seen the escaped convict," Miss St. Cloud said. "But that means we missed the whole beginning of the book. That's one of my favorite parts."

"Oh, maybe Uncle Dan can rewind it or something," Carter said. "Uncle Dan?"

His uncle's deep voice didn't speak in his ear. Carter frowned and repeated the call, but no one answered.

"That's just weird," he said. "Uncle Dan should be monitoring this."

"Daniel?" Miss St. Cloud said. "Do you hear me?"

No voice spoke.

"Well," she said, "it seems the system isn't quite as safe and secure as your uncle said."

"He said it was safe from outside hacking," Carter said loyally. "This must be something else. It *is* still in the prototype phase."

"Well, what do you do when you lose contact?" she asked.

"We can just work our way through the book," Carter said. "When we get to the end, it should let us out. Or we might find one of the backdoor exits as we go. I found one before so I think I know the kind of thing to look for."

She sighed. "Well, you're the expert, Carter. I'm in your hands. But let's look around the cemetery just for fun. This really is one of my favorite parts of the book."

Carter could think of lots of places he'd rather be than a cemetery, especially after the last book cemetery he'd gone into with Isabelle.

"Are you sure this cemetery doesn't have ghosts?" he asked.

"I'm sure," she said. "It just has a couple escaped convicts."

"Oh, that's comforting."

"Do you want me to go first?" she asked.

"No, I'm good," he said, feeling the heat in his face from knowing she must think of him as a scared kid. *Just remember,* he told himself firmly, *there are no ghosts in this book.*

The moonlight let him see the headstones clearly enough to avoid falling over them, but it didn't help much with the uneven ground. The thought that he was walking on dead people, no matter how far underground they were, made him nervous.

Trees hunched over the graves here and there, throwing pools of dark shadows where they blocked the moonlight. They also sent roots throughout the graveyard, making the ground even more uneven.

"Dickens said these roots and brambles

were like the hands of dead people stretching cautiously out of their graves to catch hold of your ankle and pull you down," Miss St. Cloud said softly.

Carter shivered, wishing she hadn't shared that particular part of the book. His eyes now stayed fixed on the ground as he stepped across each grave. He saw plenty of roots and brambles and stepped around them carefully.

Then he reached a grave where the mound rose slightly—as if it was a younger grave. The gravestone too stood straight and tall. No creeping bramble littered the ground there. Carter wondered if someone had cleared it or if weeds just hadn't had a chance to start yet.

He stepped one long leg over the mounded earth. A white hand burst through the soft soil and grabbed for his ankle. The fingernails were long and caked with dirt. A scrap of tattered lace clung to the sleeve around the horrible hand's wrist. Carter shrieked and tried to scramble backward, tripping and falling on his rear in the middle of another grave.

Two hands broke through the soil near his right arm. No flesh clung to either bony hand, though a gold ring circled one finger. Still shrieking, Carter scrambled off the grave and onto his feet. It was then that he heard Miss St. Cloud scream.

He spun and saw her. She'd fallen onto a grave as well. A bony hand, missing its pinky finger, clutched a handful of her hair and yanked her head against the ground. Carter rushed to her side and picked up a shard of broken headstone. He slammed it again and again against the bony fist until the fingers simply fell away from the palm and began twitching in the dirt like bony worms.

Then Carter hauled Miss St. Cloud to her feet and dragged her back the way they had come. He picked a last stray finger out of her hair and threw it off to one side. Soon, they were running as fast as they could through the clusters of stones. Now and then, another hand broke through the dirt and grasped at air as they passed, but nothing grabbed them again.

Finally, they reached the low church wall and scrambled over it. They stood in the narrow dirt lane, panting. Carter turned to her and asked, "Was that in the book?"

She shook her head, her face pale and dirt streaked in the moonlight. "No," she said. "And if that was just a glitch, I'd like to see a real problem."

Carter shook his head. He was afraid she was likely to get her wish before they got out of this book.

DOUBTS ARISE

"**O**kay," Miss St. Cloud said. She stood and smoothed her hair, shoving it up under her badly damaged bonnet. "What do we do now?"

"Uncle Dan and Isabelle will be wondering why they can't reach us," Carter said. "By now, they're working on a way to get us out of here. We need to stay out of trouble until then."

"I thought we were supposed to find the end of the book," she said.

"Yeah, before the zombie hands. Who knows what else this book has lurking around?"

"Maybe we should do both," she said. "We can try to stay out of trouble while working our way through the book."

Carter thought about it. He really didn't see

a better choice. Even if they hid out somewhere, the book could send the zombies in after them. "Okay."

Miss St. Cloud looked up and down the lane. "I think the village is that way about a mile," she said, pointing. "It's a nice, quiet village. We can find someplace warm to sit down."

As they walked along the rutted road, a chill wind seemed to push them along from behind. It howled through the trees that lined the road.

"There aren't any werewolves in this book, are there?" Carter asked.

"No," she said. "But then the hands in the churchyard were just a figure of speech, not bones grabbing people."

"Are there any werewolf metaphors?"

"No," she said. "I'm not sure if Dickens knew about werewolves."

"Well, that's good." Carter tried to shove his hands into his pants pockets, only to find the smooth, close-fitting pants didn't have pockets. He sighed. He probably should be glad they weren't knickers.

"Do you still think this is a glitch in the program?" Miss St. Cloud asked.

"I don't know what to think," Carter replied. "If Uncle Dan said his system was isolated from the rest of the world, I believe him. That means the hacker had to break in his house."

"Maybe he did," she said.

"Did Uncle Dan show you his security?" Carter asked. "My uncle is security crazy. His backups have backups. I guess someone could break in, but I don't believe they could do it without Uncle Dan knowing."

"Then this is a result of the last attack," she said.

Carter had to admit that seemed likely. Uncle Dan said he went through all the code, but Carter just didn't see a lot of other choices.

"Unless your cousin is doing it," Miss St. Cloud said.

"My cousin?" Carter yelped. "You mean Isabelle? You're kidding."

Miss St. Cloud shook her head. "Anyone could see she was feeling left out. Daniel said she has called him a half dozen times a day. She could have physically put a flash drive into one of the computers and downloaded some kind of virus. We weren't really watching her."

"Isabelle wouldn't do something like that," Carter said, but even he could tell his voice didn't sound sure. His cousin was hurt about being cut out after all they'd done to help their uncle. And she could certainly come up with the needed software. She was almost as brilliant as Uncle Dan.

Carter didn't even like thinking about it. He picked up his pace. For a while, they just walked in the darkness. They began to see small houses, though Carter might have classified them more as "shacks." Each building was dark.

"Must be late," he said.

"Not necessarily," Miss St. Cloud answered. "Without electricity, most poor people went to bed early. It was cheaper than paying for candles or lamp oil. It's almost Christmas here and night comes early."

Carter scuffed at the stray rocks in the hard-packed dirt of the lane. Houses were popping up closer and closer together. Carter thought they must be heading into the village. "So if everyone is asleep, what are we going to do? Just stand around and wait for morning?"

"Not everyone will be asleep," Miss St. Cloud said. "Not in the village itself and not this close to Christmas."

"It doesn't look much like Christmas," Carter said as he peered at another dreary shack.

"This was a time before twinkle lights," Miss St. Cloud said. "And for most of the people, if you had money to celebrate Christmas at all, you spent it on food, not decorations."

Carter just grunted. He never knew what to say when an adult told him how easy modern kids had it. Sure, he didn't have to do homework by candlelight or kill chickens for supper, but sometimes his life was pretty hard. Still, there was never any point in arguing with old people.

As he looked around, he noticed that it was getting easier and easier to make out details in the clusters of homes they passed. Not every house was dark anymore.

"We're coming into the village," she said. "We should start seeing more people."

And sure enough, a few minutes later they began to come to groups of people standing on wooden sidewalks. Although the streets were still gloomy, they were no longer dark. Carter suspected the program was giving them extra light so they could enjoy the story more.

Too bad it doesn't give us an exit, he thought. *I'd enjoy that a lot.*

That's when Carter noticed something really weird. The people all stopped as soon as Carter and Miss St. Cloud grew close. They didn't speak but they stared.

"Why are they staring at us?" Carter whispered.

Miss St. Cloud shrugged. "We're strangers.

They're probably curious."

They didn't look curious, he thought. They looked angry. He cleared his throat nervously. "Now that we're in the village, what do we do?"

"We should find the blacksmith shop," she said. "That's where Pip's uncle works. It should be a safe place to plan our next move."

"Where is the blacksmith shop?" he asked.

"I don't know." She stopped and looked up and down the street. "Maybe we should ask someone." She strode toward the sidewalk where a small cluster of old women stood staring at them.

As soon as it was clear Miss St. Cloud was heading their way, the women turned and hustled into the building beside them. Miss St. Cloud tried to follow, but the door was locked. She pounded on the rough wood, but no sound came from inside.

They continued down the lane. Carter tried to approach the next group, a tight knot of men leaning on the wall of a building. The sign dangling from a post proclaimed it the *Three Jolly Bargemen*. Though none of the men staring at Carter looked the least bit jolly. As soon as they realized he was heading directly to them, they turned and went into the pub. Carter tried to follow, but again the door wouldn't open.

"Who locks up a pub?" he asked.

Miss St. Cloud shook her head, her face lined with worry. "I don't like this."

"If they turn into zombies, I'm out of here."

"Let's just keep looking."

They walked down the lane, turning sometimes to go up side streets. Finally Miss St. Cloud's face lit up. "Do you smell that?" she asked.

Carter took a deep breath. He smelled metal. It was sharp, fresh, and almost tangy like the smell of iron in blood. "Like blood?"

"That's the smell of hot iron," she said grinning. "I had iron work done for a gate once. I know that smell. The forge is close."

They followed their noses to a wooden house

with a roughly built extension that reeked of hot metal. They had found the forge.

"Good," Miss St. Cloud said. "Now things are looking up."

They walked in through the public door of the forge, but no one stood inside near the fire.

"Joe?" Miss St. Cloud whispered. It was clear she didn't trust this weird book world anymore than Carter did.

"The forge connects to the house," she whispered to Carter. "We should be able to just walk through."

They found the door at the back of the forge and pushed it silently open. They could see into the kitchen of the house now. A thin woman with coal black hair lay sprawled on the floor, blood pooling next to her head.

A man stood over her with an iron tool in his hand. He looked up at them, and Miss St. Cloud whispered, "Dolge Orlick!"

His scowl turned fierce. Holding the tool over his head, he rushed right at them.

SATIS HOUSE

For a moment, Miss St. Cloud stood staring as the blacksmith lurched toward them. Carter grabbed her arm and dragged her away.

"Why are we running?" she asked.

"Because he's chasing," Carter said, pulling harder to get her to move faster.

Finally she gave in. She grabbed her skirt to lift the hem above her shoes and ran. Relief flooded Carter as he sprinted along beside her. For a while, they heard the heavy footsteps of Orlick behind them, but eventually that faded.

Rain began to fall in fat drops. *Because this wasn't fun enough*, Carter thought gloomily as a raindrop dripped off his nose.

They ducked around a few more corners.

Finally, they half collapsed against a strong brick wall and gasped for several minutes.

"Why," Miss St. Cloud panted, "did we run?"

"Because he had a crowbar and liked bashing people in the head." *Adults ask the stupidest questions sometimes*, Carter thought.

Miss St. Cloud shook her head, flinging icy drops of water at Carter. "I mean, why run? Didn't your uncle say you couldn't really get hurt in here? None of this is real."

Carter took her hand and put it against the cold, damp brick walls. "Does that feel real?"

"Yes, but it's not hurting me," she said.

"It would if it bashed you in the head. I've been in these books when they've gone crazy. They can definitely hurt you. And that Orlick guy wanted to kill us."

"You don't think your cousin would put anything in this that would kill someone, do you?" She stared at him in disbelief. "I mean, I know she doesn't like me and all . . ."

"Izzy wouldn't hurt us," Carter said firmly.

"And I don't know that Izzy is doing this."

"Have you heard of Occam's razor?" Miss St. Cloud asked.

"Why, does someone run around in this book and cut throats with it?" he asked, horrified. "Because I'm really beginning to think you made a terrible choice in books."

She waved off his complaint. "It's not a real razor, it's a logical concept. It says that when you eliminate the impossible, what you have left is your answer—even if it seems unlikely."

"Isabelle trying to hurt us is the impossible," Carter said. "And so is her wanting to ruin Uncle Dan's project. We've worked too hard to save it."

"No one can get to this system from the outside," Miss St. Cloud said. "Your uncle told us that. You agreed. So this is an inside job."

Carter shook his head. His cousin wasn't doing this. He wouldn't believe it.

"Look, let's just get out of here," Carter said. "It's daytime. Where should we go?"

"I don't even know where we are," she said.

Carter looked around. He hadn't exactly drawn a map while they were running. The street was pounded dirt like the others, but most of the buildings were brick instead of wood. He didn't know what that meant.

"I guess we walk until something comes up," he said. "Who knows? Maybe we'll find the exit to the program. Last time, the exit was a skinny door with an *x* carved into the wood."

Miss St. Cloud wiped water out of her face and looked around. "So we start checking doors?" she asked.

"I guess," Carter answered.

They trudged down the street, splashing muddy water onto already soggy clothes. Carter's feet felt uncomfortably squishy in his shoes. Every time they came to a door in any of the buildings, they tried to open it. None would open.

"This isn't exactly a friendly village," Carter grumbled.

"We need to get out of this rain," Miss St. Cloud said. "I don't know how the suits are keeping us so wet, but it can't be healthy."

"I'm not seeing a lot of options for places to go," he said.

"That better change soon."

They stumbled on and eventually came to a tall fence with a grimy brick house beyond. Even with the rain, Carter could see many of the windows in the house were walled up. Others had iron bars. Carter wondered if they were to keep things out or keep things in.

"I know this place," Miss St. Cloud said as she stopped and wiped water from her face again. "This is Satis House. It's where Miss Havisham lives."

"Is she friendly?" Carter asked.

"No, she's insane. But since she's part of the story, maybe we can get in. I think they keep the gate barred, but there's a bell."

They hurried to the heavy gate. Carter saw the heavy bell hanging beside it. He reached up to ring it when he realized the gate hung open slightly. "It's not locked," he said.

"That's strange," she answered. "Miss Havisham wouldn't leave the gate open."

"That sounds like a good reason for us not to go in there," Carter answered. "I've seen enough women with their heads bashed in for one day."

"We don't have a choice," Miss St. Cloud said. "We need to get out of this rain."

She pushed the gate. It swung open with a rusty groan. Carter had never wanted to go somewhere less than he wanted to go through that gate, but he couldn't let Miss St. Cloud go alone.

They walked into a small courtyard where sickly weeds grew up between the bricks. Miss St. Cloud pointed at part of the building that looked like an old factory. "That was a brewery."

"Doesn't look like they've brewed anything there for a long time," he said.

"No, not for a long time."

Finally, they reached a door on the side of

the building. Miss St. Cloud raised a knocker to pound it against the wood. The doorway was sheltered slightly from the rain. Carter wiped his face with his sleeve and pushed his hair away from his face. He appreciated being able to see, even if it didn't make him feel any drier.

They waited so long that Carter suggested they give up and move on twice. Miss St. Cloud just ignored him. Finally, they heard the sound of locks turning and a board being slid away. The door opened on a girl near Carter's age with brown curls. She would have been pretty, but her eyes were cold and her lips were pinched together. Overall, Carter thought she looked stuck up.

"What do you want?" the girl asked.

"Shelter from the rain," Miss St. Cloud answered.

"We don't accept visitors at Satis House," the girl said with small smile. She began to close the door.

Miss St. Cloud reached out to lean against

the door, shoving her booted foot into the crack before it could close. "Tell Miss Havisham that I tell fortunes. Wouldn't she like to know what the future holds for her? Wouldn't you?"

The girl sniffed. "I know what the future holds for her."

"But that's not for you to say, is it? Go and ask your mistress if she wants to hear, Estella."

The girl looked surprised. "How do you know my name?"

"I know many things," Miss St. Cloud said mysteriously. "I know that Miss Havisham dresses you like a doll. I know about her cake and her clothes. I know of the ambition in your heart. Don't you want to know what I see?"

"I don't care," Estella cried. Still, she backed away from the crack in the door. "I will ask Miss Havisham if she wishes to see you. You can wait inside for her answer."

The girl led them into a small parlor where a fire flickered in a tiny fireplace. "Stay here."

She walked out of the room. Carter checked

all the doors for suspicious markings. None looked like the exit they needed. Finally he walked to the fireplace, enjoying the heat.

"You did great with the fortune telling thing," he said.

"I do know their future," Miss St. Cloud said. "I've read this book."

"I'll have to keep that trick in mind," Carter said, then he shivered. "I would sure appreciate a dry change of clothes."

Miss St. Cloud just nodded. She took off her ruined bonnet and hung it on a hook next to the fireplace. Then she quickly squeezed water from her hair and braided it.

The door to the small parlor creaked open and Estella came in, carrying a candle. "Come with me. Miss Havisham will see you."

Miss St. Cloud hurried toward the door. Carter reluctantly followed. He had the creeping feeling that he was not going to like whatever came next in this book.

No Exit

They walked through a twisting maze of narrow hallways, all of them dark. The tiny pool of light thrown by Estella's candle did little to help Carter make out any details. Each time they walked by a door, he ran his hand over the surface, checking for marks that might suggest an exit. As a result, he fell farther and farther behind Estella and Miss St. Cloud.

The young girl turned and snapped at him. "Do keep up. Or are you trying to pretend to be starved and weak? One look at you makes that a lie."

Carter scowled. "Well, aren't you rude?"

Finally, the girl smiled a little. "Yes," she said. "I am rude. And you're common!"

She stopped in front of a door that looked much like all the other doors they had passed.

She opened it and gestured for them to enter.

The room was larger than the small parlor where they had waited. Wax candles sat on most of the bare surfaces, giving off enough light to see. Heavy drapes covered the windows. Carter wondered if the windows behind the drapes were bricked over.

The room seemed crowded with half-packed trunks, now covered with dust. An incredibly thin woman sat in an armchair. Her head rested in her hand. She peered at them for a moment before finally standing. She was dressed in an ancient dress, yellow and brittle with wear. The dress must have once been impressive with plenty of lace and fancy fabric, but now it hung loosely on her thin body.

The woman wore a long, white veil and dead, dry flowers were woven into her white hair. She wore fancy jewelry with rings on every bony finger. She had on one white shoe.

The woman looked withered and dried like the flowers in her hair. Her hands reminded

Carter of the first pair of writhing bony hands that had burst from the grave in the cemetery. For a moment, Carter wondered if this was the woman in that grave, now crawled all the way out and waiting for them.

"Miss Havisham," Miss St. Cloud said, "I am pleased to meet you."

The old woman narrowed her eyes at Miss St. Cloud. "Estella says you have second sight."

"I do," Miss St. Cloud said. "And I can tell you much. But first we need hot food and dry clothes."

"You ask for a lot to share what might be worthless," the old woman said.

"I know you wear the gown you wore when you received the note from your lover," Miss St. Cloud said. "The note that told you he would not marry you. I know you have vowed revenge on young men. I know Estella is meant to be the instrument of that revenge."

The old woman's sunken eyes sparked. "Ah, you do have things to say to me. Okay, Estella, take the fortune-teller to the kitchen and bring trays of supper. Then find them clothes. Something of my father's might fit the young man. He can wait here with me and keep me company."

Estella nodded. Carter didn't like the idea of staying behind with the zombie lady, but he didn't know how to say something without sounding like a wimp.

"So, boy," the old woman said, "what is your name?"

"Carter," he said. "Carter Lewis."

"Give me your arm then, Carter," she said. "I would like to walk while we wait for them."

"I'm all wet," he said.

"And afraid of a frail, old woman?"

He shook his head, even though he was a little scared. He stepped closer and she latched onto his arm like a vulture, her long nails digging into his arm like talons.

"I have a room I like to walk in across the hall," she said. "Let's go there."

"Will they be able to find us?" he asked. His voice sounded a little squeaky in his ears.

"Estella will know. I only go between the two rooms. It is my whole world."

They walked together across the hall to a much larger room. No daylight entered that room either, and it had fewer candles. Vast pools of darkness lay in the corners of the room. A fire burned in the fireplace grate. The chimney must have been partially blocked, because the room smelled smoky and musty. Another smell hung in the air, but Carter didn't recognize it.

The old woman sunk her claws deeper into Carter's arm and urged him toward the long table in the center of the room. A tablecloth stained with patches of dampness and mold covered the table.

Something sat in the center of the table, but Carter had trouble telling what it was. The thing was covered with cobwebs and Carter could see a fat, black spider skittering along them. Now and then, a mouse darted out of the mess and ran down the cloth to leap to the floor.

"This," the old woman said, "is where I will be laid when I am dead. They shall come and look at me here."

"You know," Carter said as he began prying the claws out of his arm. "You probably shouldn't dwell on stuff like that."

"Do you think me mad, boy?" she asked, digging her fingers deeper.

"I think you need to get outside more and maybe cut your fingernails," he said.

The old woman pointed at the table. "Do you know what that is?"

"The world's ugliest centerpiece?"

"It is my bride cake," she said. "Mine."

"Wow, you ration your junk food a lot better than I do," he said. He finally gave up on getting her claws out of his arm and decided to try a distraction. "I thought you wanted to walk."

"Walk," she screeched. "Walk!"

They began a slow stroll around the dark,

smelly room. Carter began to wish the virtual reality suits weren't quite so good at smell-o-vision.

"Do you find Estella beautiful?" the old woman asked.

"I find her snotty," he said.

"You must love her!" she commanded.

"Okay, that's it," Carter yelled. The suddenness of his shout must have startled Miss Havisham. She let go of his arm, and he backed away from her. "This is just too weird. You tell Miss St. Cloud that I'm looking for the exit."

He spun and charged out of the room, rubbing his sore arm. He decided he'd just find Miss St. Cloud and they could leave this crazy place. There had to be a better place to get out of the rain than this. He might even like running from Orlick better than this.

Carter stomped down each corridor and turned corners, searching for the staircase down. At first, he was just reminded of how maze-like the place was. Then he noticed that he passed a door slightly cracked in each hallway over and over.

Carter stopped and peeked into one of the slightly open doors. He saw the gloomy room and the moldy wedding cake. He jumped back. "How did I get back here?"

He turned and ran down the hall, turning sharply at the corner and sprinting down the next hall. Then he staggered to a stop at a slightly open door. He looked in and found himself face-to-face with Miss Havisham. Carter turned and ran down the hall, turning another corner and finding himself right back to the open door.

How was he going to find Miss St. Cloud if he couldn't even get out of the hall?

SETTLING IN FOR THE NIGHT

Carter leaned against the wall, panting. He didn't care how stubborn the program was acting. He was not going back into the room with the weird old lady and the moldy cake.

Then he caught sight of a faint light coming from down the hall. "Hello?" he yelled, but no one answered. The light grew slowly brighter until Estella turned the corner, carrying a candle.

"Why didn't you answer when I called?" he asked.

"Yelling down the hallway is common," she said with a sniff.

He assumed being "common" was bad since she was acting all prissy about it. "Fine," he snapped. "How do I get out of this hallway?"

She looked at him oddly. "Walk?"

"I tried that," he said. "I tried running, too."

She sniffed again. "I wouldn't know about running."

Carter rolled his eyes. This girl was seriously a pain. She was enough to make him think fond thoughts of Isabelle.

"I will show you to a room for the night," Estella said. Her tone of voice showed just how much she did not want to show him anything at all. "Follow me."

"Where's Miss St. Cloud?"

"She has already been shown to her room," Estella said. "Follow me."

Carter considered refusing just because the girl had such a bad attitude, but he didn't want to be stuck in the creepy old lady hallway anymore. So he grumbled quietly as he followed Estella.

He looked around in the gloomy halls as they walked. He could tell they were no longer stuck in the single hallway.

Finally, they came to a stairway, and Estella led him down one level. Now the hall was even more narrow. She stopped before a door.

"This will be your room," she said as she swung the door open. The room was small and faintly lit. A candle rested on the table by the bed. It gave off just enough glow that Carter could see a change of clothes lying on the bed.

"Where is Miss St. Cloud?" he asked.

"She is in her room," Estella answered.

"Yeah," he snapped. "I know. Where is it?"

Estella looked shocked. "It is not appropriate to disturb a woman in her room."

"I know, but I'm common, remember?" he said. "Where is her room?"

When Estella seemed ready to refuse to tell him, he added, "Do you really want to stand here and argue with me all night?"

Clearly she did not. "It's that one," she inclined her head toward the door across the hall. "Good night. I hope you will be gone in the morning!" She turned and strode down the hall as quickly as she could without running.

Carter made a rude noise after her, then walked across and knocked on the rough wooden door. When Miss St. Cloud opened it, Carter could see she had changed her clothes.

"We seem to be in the servant's quarters," she said.

"At least they don't come with moldy wedding cake," he answered.

"Oh, you got to see the cake?" Miss St. Cloud said. "That's one of my favorite parts of the book. Was it creepy?"

"Definitely," he said. "Though I think Miss Havisham might be creepier."

Miss St. Cloud laughed. "She's one of my favorite characters in literature. She has inspired so many writers since then."

In Carter's opinion, writers must be strange people if they found that inspiring. "We need to talk."

She raised her eyebrows at his serious tone, but simply backed into the room and gestured for him to follow. The room was small and almost a mirror image of his. Beside the bed, a small table held a single candle. Somehow Carter didn't feel right sitting on the bed beside Miss St. Cloud, so he just leaned on the door.

"There's no way that this is some weird glitch," he said. "Since it wasn't Isabelle, that means we've been hacked. And that means Storm wants something."

"Storm?"

"That's what the hacker calls himself."

"Oh," she said. "What does he want?"

"He wants to stop or delay Uncle Dan's invention," Carter said. "He's working on one of his own."

"Do you think he's a character in this book?" she asked.

Carter shook his head. "There's no one we're seeing consistently. It's also weird that we're not seeing storm clues."

"Storm clues?" she asked.

"Well, this guy is kind of full of himself. So

when he wasn't in the program himself, he stuck in weird storm clues. Characters talked about storms all the time, but there hasn't been any of that here."

"We did get rained on," she said.

He nodded, but somehow that didn't seem extreme enough. "Plain old rain could just happen because it's a gloomy book. It wasn't a tornado or something really big. Storm seems to like being noticed."

"Maybe this isn't about him being noticed," she said. "What if it's something else."

"Well, we're trapped in here and cut off from Uncle Dan and Isabelle," Carter said. "We're just running around in circles. All we're doing is wearing ourselves out."

"If we did that long enough, we'd get sick," she said. "Exhaustion for sure, maybe even dehydration or something worse."

"Oh no," Carter sagged against the wall thinking about it. "What if that's what Storm wants? You're here to maybe invest in the invention. If we're stuck in the suits until you get sick or worse, the investment wouldn't happen."

"It definitely wouldn't," she said dryly. "And what about you? You're just a kid. If you ended up in the hospital, no one would touch this thing. Not any investor."

Carter shook his head. "Uncle Dan won't let that happen. Even if he can't see us or talk to us, he would be suspicious if we just never come out of the suits. Eventually he'll get us out, because he knows it's getting dangerous."

"What if he makes that call based on a normal amount of physical effort?" she said. "We've been running a lot. We're going to feel the bad effect of that a lot sooner. Maybe we should just sit still and wait for your uncle to shut the system down.

Carter nodded. "That makes sense. This house is creepy, but we're out of the rain. We could just sit it out. As long as I don't have to take any more walks with that old lady."

As he said that, a vicious banging noise began from down the hall. It sounded as if someone were pounding on the walls with some huge hammer. The pounding made the floor under Carter's feet vibrate.

"So, is there supposed to be pounding in this book?" he asked.

She shook her head.

"Super," he answered. "Well, at least it's out there. Maybe we should just stay in here out of trouble."

The words were barely out of his mouth when pounding sounded against the wall. Then the wardrobe next to the wall began to rattle. The wardrobe door banged open and the broad-shouldered blacksmith's apprentice stumbled out.

"You saw me," he whispered hoarsely. "You saw what I did."

THE DOORWAY

The man raised a long, metal bar and lurched toward them.

Carter jerked the room door open. He stumbled into the hall with Miss St. Cloud right behind him. Carter looked up and down the hall, but it was empty. Miss St. Cloud grabbed his arm and half dragged him down the hall to the left.

"We have to find the end program exit," Carter yelled as they ran. They could hear Orlick's pounding feet behind them, along with the crash of the metal bar against the wall.

"We've been looking for an exit," Miss St. Cloud gasped.

"Maybe there's an end program exit near the end of the book. If we go to that spot, it might be easier to get out. Where does *Great*

Expectations end?"

"Here," she said. "At Satis House. Actually, outside in the garden."

"Then we need to get outside."

"Sounds good to me."

They ran down hallway after hallway. Orlick never seemed to gain on them, but they couldn't shake him off either. As soon as they paused, they would hear the slamming crash of his iron bar against a wall or door.

Finally they came to a narrow set of stairs. "Up or down?" Carter asked. "I'm not sure how to get outside."

"These are servant stairs," Miss St. Cloud panted, pushing by Carter to begin clattering down the steps. "They'll lead to the kitchen and there should be a door leading outside."

That reasoning sounded good to Carter, especially when he heard Orlick bellow from somewhere close behind him. He charged down the stairs. They came out in a large, dusty kitchen. Wherever meals were made for Satis

House, this wasn't it. But there was an outside door, and they ran to it. Two loud crashes on the narrow stairs helped with their speed.

Finally, they stumbled outside. Carter spotted a large barrel not far away and rolled it to the door. Then, he wedged the top rim of the barrel under the doorknob.

"Where now?" he asked.

"The gardens," Miss St. Cloud said, her voice still high and wheezy. "At the end of the book, Pip comes to Satis House. It's just a ruin and he finds Estella in the garden."

Carter nodded. "But we need to be careful. The house wouldn't let me out before, so I'm wondering why it was so easy to get out now."

Miss St. Cloud looked around them nervously. "You think something new is waiting out here?"

"Or more of something old," he said. "Hey, it's daylight out here."

Miss St. Cloud looked around. "Yes, though it's so cloudy and dismal. It's hard to tell what time of day it is."

"It was night when we were upstairs," he said. "Remember, we were spending the night? Time is all scrambled up in this book."

Miss St. Cloud nodded. "We're jumping around in the book. Plus, Orlick never rampaged through Satis House with an iron bar."

Miss St. Cloud headed toward the walled garden where a rugged wooden door stood open. Inside, the garden clearly had not seen a gardener in a long time. Weeds and vines grew together in a tangle over wooden frames that must once have been for vegetables.

Near the far wall, an empty greenhouse covered nothing but a grape vine. The frame that once held it up had decayed and the grape vine trailed on the floor as if reaching out for help.

As they turned and walked out of the greenhouse, they found someone standing in the middle of the garden. The pale, thin young man seemed about Carter's age. His clothes were well made but worn.

"Halloo!" the boy said. "Who told you two you could prowl around?"

"We're looking for an exit," Carter said.

The boy looked confused for a moment, then said, "Come and fight!"

Carter looked over the pale, skinny boy facing him. "It wouldn't be fair. I'm taller than you and probably stronger. I really don't want to fight."

The boy clapped his hands, then one pale hand darted out quickly. For a moment, Carter thought the boy was trying to slap him. Instead, he just grabbed a handful of Carter's hair and pulled.

"Hey!" Carter yelped.

Then the boy bent over and headbutted Carter in the stomach, knocking Carter on the ground.

Carter scrambled up quickly. "Is everyone crazy in this book?" he asked.

"He just likes to fight," Miss St. Cloud said.

"Well, I don't want to." Carter gave the thinner boy a push, then he turned and began to walk away. "We need to find the doorway out of here."

"Oh, you should have said that," the thin boy said. "I can show you."

"We want to get all the way out of here. Out of this garden, out of this town, out of this program!"

"Program?" the boy looked confused again. "There's a door over here."

He led them to a narrow wooden door near the farthest corner of the garden wall. It was partially hidden by overgrown vines. The boy began tugging at the vines. Carter joined him, but for every strand they pulled away, another seemed to spring back.

"That must be the exit," Miss St. Cloud said. "Whatever the hacker did is trying to keep us in."

"Maybe you can squeeze around the vines," the thin boy said. He stuck his hand through a gap in the vines and must have grasped a door handle because Carter heard the rusty protest of metal on metal.

"It's open," Miss St. Cloud said, peering through the vines. "I'm squeezing through." Though a fairly tall woman, she was more slender than Carter. Still, it took considerable squeezing and twisting to get through the vines. Finally, she disappeared from sight.

"Is that it?" Carter yelled. "Are you through?"

He didn't hear any answer, but since the communication with the suits wasn't working, not hearing anything from her might be a good sign. "I just wish we could get these vines loose," he said, pulling again at the clinging vine.

Suddenly, he heard a roar and a crash. Carter and the pale boy turned sharply. Orlick stood near the greenhouse, his iron bar half buried in the broken greenhouse glass.

"You better go," the boy said. "I'll hold him off. I'm an excellent fighter."

He grabbed Carter's arm and pushed him

hard at the tangle of vines. Leaves and twigs slapped at his face as the boy shoved him. Suddenly, the vines seemed to shift. Carter found himself tumbling through and into the darkness.

For a moment, Carter thought he'd made it. But the darkness was only night. He was on his hands and knees on a brick road. Miss St. Cloud offered him her hand and hauled him to his feet. "Where are we?"

"I believe it's London," she said. "Part of the novel takes place in London."

"Terrific," Carter mumbled. At least it wasn't raining.

The streets were busy, despite the late hour, and they had to step out of the way of horse-drawn wagons and even one black carriage. Street lamps threw puddles of light on the sidewalks at the street corners.

As people passed them on the bustling sidewalks, no one paid them much attention. "I think I like London a lot better than the Village of the Creeps."

"So far," Miss St. Cloud said.

"I smell fish and wet yuck," he said.

"We must be near the docks," she said.

"Does any of the book take place on the water?" Carter asked.

She nodded. "Quite a bit."

"Does it involve any zombies, bony old ladies in wedding gowns, or guys with iron bars?" he asked.

"No," she told him.

Good, he thought. He'd had enough of the creepy stuff. He just wanted to get out of there. First, he was going to have at least one soda, maybe two. Then food. Uncle Dan was home, so that meant his fridge would be packed with what Uncle Dan considered brain food—mostly things Carter's mother would never let him eat.

They passed through more streets and more bustle. Soon, Carter could hear the sounds of the docks. The creak and groan of wood straining as the huge ships bobbed in the water.

The sound of feet on wood.

"We should be careful," Miss St. Cloud said. "Dock workers can be rough."

They slipped around quietly as they finally got within sight of the ships and docks. They kept piles of wooden crates and small shacks and sheds between themselves and the men working close to the water.

They walked along the shoreline, not speaking. Carter couldn't see how there could be an exit anywhere along there. To have a door, you need to have a wall. Of course, the sheds had doors, but none of them looked likely and more hung half agape.

The crowd grew thinner as they moved away from the large ships. Finally, they heard the sounds of muffled voices just ahead. So far, everyone they'd seen was either completely silent or shouting to be heard above the bustle of work. The quiet voices seemed secretive and suspicious to Carter. He exchanged a silent glance with Miss St. Cloud. They walked closer, slowly and quietly.

Finally, through a gap between two shipping crates, they spotted two young men creeping along, murmuring to one another. Carter stepped through the crack between the boxes. He realized one of the young men looked familiar. He recognized him as an older version of the boy in the garden who wanted to fight.

"Wow," Carter said. "We've really jumped ahead in this book."

At the sound of his voice, both young men jumped and turned to stare at Carter.

"What do you want?" the unfamiliar man said.

"Nothing, Pip," Miss St. Cloud said.

"Pip?" the young man's face darkened and he strode toward them. "How do you know my name. I don't know you."

"I saw you once," she said. "When you were just a little boy running out of a cemetery."

Pip shook his head. "You'd be an old woman now. I don't know what game you're playing, but you better tell me the truth."

Both young men stalked toward them, their faces grim.

"Look," Carter said as he backed away with his hands up, "we don't want any trouble."

"Why are you spying on us?" Pip asked. "Who sent you?"

"No one sent us," Carter tried. "We didn't mean to spy. We were just out for a walk."

"A lady walking in the dark on the docks," Pip said with a laugh. "An interesting choice of exercise."

Carter continued to back away. He noticed Miss St. Cloud stood fixed, as if delighted to be face-to-face with these characters from her favorite book. Carter reached out to snatch at her arm. Without even looking at him, she took a step toward the two men.

"Maybe we can help you," she said. "We can help you get your friend away."

This seemed to upset the two men still more and Carter started to wonder if she was trying to get them killed. As he tried to decide how to calm everyone down when he had no idea what was going on, he got the biggest surprise of all.

"Carter?" a voice said in his ear.

Without making a sound, Carter's lips formed the word, "Isabelle."

Izzy to the Rescue

Carter stood frozen in place, barely aware that the two men on the dock were still talking to Miss St. Cloud. He couldn't believe his cousin had finally gotten through to them. He took a deep breath to ask her exactly what took her so long, when she spoke again.

"Carter," Isabelle said, "if you're anywhere near that woman, don't talk. Just run. You need to get somewhere alone so I can talk to you."

Carter blinked and looked around. Where to go? Suddenly, the young man who had wanted to fight at Satis House grabbed him by the arm. "You better come with us," he said.

This time Carter decided a little bit of violence might be appropriate. He felt a little bad about it, since the guy had been willing to fight Orlick. He reminded himself that this was just a digital image in a program. He shoved the young man hard in the chest. The young man stumbled backward, got caught in a discarded pile of rope, and fell on his rear.

"Hey!" Pip yelled. "That's enough of that."

Not knowing what else to do, Carter spun and ran. "Carter, what are you doing?" Miss St. Cloud called after him. But Carter just ran harder. He knew he should be able to outrun her easily. He was every bit as tall as her, younger, and not wearing heavy skirts.

His feet pounded on the boards of the dock. Carter realized he needed to get away from the water so it would be harder to find him. He turned at the first street he saw, running hard up the sidewalk, pushing rudely past anyone who blocked his way. He didn't have time for manners with computer people.

Finally, he ducked into a narrow alley that smelled of cabbage and dampness. He leaned against the wall, panting. He was starting to feel like he'd been panting for hours. He leaned his head back against the cool wall and gasped, "Izzy?"

"Are you clear?"

"Yeah," he wheezed. "For now."

"Good. We found a virus in the system."

"You think?" Carter half yelled. "I've been grabbed by zombies, chased by a murderer, and seriously creeped out by an old lady with the world's grossest wedding cake."

"Huh?" Isabelle said.

"Where's Uncle Dan?"

"He went next door to call the police on their landline in case that woman has the phones bugged, too."

"Why would Miss St. Cloud bug Uncle Dan's phones?" Carter asked, totally confused.

"Because she's Storm! I was an idiot not to spot it right away. Tempest St. Cloud. Tempest. Storm. I totally understand why you and Uncle Dan didn't get it. All she had to do was look at you guys with those big, blue eyes."

"Don't even go there," Carter said. "So, you think it's her because of her name?"

"And because it had to be someone with physical access to the system," Isabelle said. "Uncle Dan wasn't kidding. You can't get in any other way. Remember how she hung around the computers? She must have been activating it then."

Carter nodded. That made sense. "So what do we do about it?"

"I'm trying to build you a back door as fast as I can," Isabelle said. "But you need to stay away from Miss St. Cloud. There's no telling what she might do if she suspects you're on to her. She may have verbal passwords set up that she can trigger inside the program."

"Making a door for me could be a problem. This program is all messed up," Carter said. "It dumps me into different places and times. No matter where you put the door, I'm going to have trouble reaching it to get out."

"Don't worry about that," Isabelle said. "I

have an idea. Trust me."

Carter frowned. He hated it when she said that. Still, he didn't know that he had any other choice. Then he jumped as he heard Miss St. Cloud calling his name from somewhere nearby.

"She's coming," he whispered. "I have to go."

"Be careful," Isabelle said.

Carter turned and ran down the alley as quickly as he could. The packed dirt under his feet grew more wet and clingy the farther he ran. Finally he burst out from between the two buildings. But instead of being on a brick street in London, he saw the marshes stretching out in front of him.

"Oh no," he moaned. "I'm back in zombieland."

It was still night and the moonlight threw a weak glow that made it fairly easy to walk, though Carter worried about quicksand. He'd seen on television that quicksand couldn't really suck you in and kill you. But he really wasn't interested in testing it, especially since anything could happen in a book.

As Carter walked, he began to smell something sharp but burnt. It smelled a little like Joe's forge but not completely. He followed the smell until he came to some kind of quarry. No one was around, though he could see fires burning down in pits.

Just then, a light rain pattered down on him. Carter groaned. He was beginning to hate English rain. In the gloom, he could see a worn wooden building with a tile roof. It was badly damaged by time and weather, but it was still standing. He walked to the door and listened.

He heard nothing inside. He wondered if the building were the office for the quarry. If so, the workmen were probably gone for the day. Carter could get in out of the rain until Izzy got him out of the book entirely.

Carter lifted the door latch and the door swung open. A single lit candle sat on a half turned crate someone used for a table. A sagging bed, a small table, and a bench completed the furniture.

Whatever building this is, Carter thought, *someone is living here.*

He picked up the candle and called out, "Hello? Is anyone home?"

Just then, a gust of wind blew out the candle. At the exact same moment, a rough rope fell over Carter's head and slipped down to his arms. The rope tightened painfully to bind his arms to his side.

"Now, I've got you," a hoarse voice rasped.

Horrified, Carter recognized the voice. It was Orlick, the murderer.

A QUICK STORM

Carter heard the sound of a flint strike, and the candle lit again. Seeing Orlick's gloating face didn't make him feel any better.

Carter yelled, "Isabelle, I need that door!"

For a moment, the surly blacksmith looked confused, but then he laughed. "No use calling for help," he said. "I'm the only one around, and I don't plan to help you none."

Orlick laughed again as Carter bellowed over and over for Isabelle. Then Orlick shoved him down on the hard bench.

"Close your yap," the killer snarled. "Any more of that, and I'll make you sorry."

"Really?" Carter said. "You don't think I know you're planning to kill me?"

"Well, there's all kinds of killing," Orlick said.

"There's the quick kind that doesn't hurt too much, and then there's the slow kind with lots of screaming. I don't like the noise myself, but I might bear it for you."

"Wow, thanks," Carter said squirming in the ropes. The rope had been pulled so tight it burned across Carter's upper arm. "Why are you set on killing me anyway?"

"You know," Orlick said, shaking a knife under Carter's nose. "You know! You saw what I did to that old shrew. She was always yelling at me. I shut her up good, and you saw."

Carter looked at him. "I'm not going to tell anyone. I just want to go home."

"I'd like to say I believe a fine young gentleman like you," Orlick said, laughing again. "But I need to help you along. I'm going to make you the best secret keeper in the marsh."

At that, Orlick howled with laughter. Carter slouched down on the bench slightly and kicked Orlick hard in the shin. Orlick dropped his knife and hopped around, howling.

Carter struggled to get to his feet, but with his arm tightly bound, he just managed to slump sideways on the bench. Finally, Orlick hobbled to the knife and picked it up.

"You're going to make good practice," he growled. "What I do to you, I'm going to do to that whiny brat Pip."

The man began to laugh again but suddenly stopped and dropped to the floor. With the broad-shouldered man on the floor, Carter could see Miss St. Cloud standing behind him, clutching the iron bar Orlick had carried earlier.

"Did you kill him?" Carter squeaked.

"He's not real," she said, kicking the body hard in the shin. "Remember? Think of it as poetic justice." She kicked the body again. When it didn't move, she bent down and picked up the knife. "He bashed Mrs. Joe, and I bashed him."

She began sawing at the rope with the knife. Carter yelped, "Be careful with that. I'm not digital!"

"I'll try not to cut your arm off," she said.

"Thanks."

Finally the ropes fell away. Miss St. Cloud stood in front of him with her hands on her hips. "Didn't you hear me calling you? I had a terrible time finding the door in that alley. What would you have done if I hadn't gotten here in time?"

"I guess all of this just caught up to me at once," Carter lied. "I got scared. I'm just a kid you know."

She looked at him skeptically. Clearly she wasn't buying it.

"All that doesn't matter," she said finally. "We need to stick together now. Who knows what other surprises your cousin has hidden in this book. Clearly she doesn't care who gets hurt."

Carter frowned. "Isabelle wouldn't want me hurt."

"Are you so sure?"

For a moment, Carter wasn't. If Miss St.

94

Cloud was really the hacker, why did she save him from Orlick? Wouldn't it be better for Storm's plan to let the blacksmith hurt him? Still, the only other possibility was that Isabelle really didn't care if he was hurt or even killed.

Isabelle was stubborn and irritating and a total know-it-all, but Carter knew that family mattered to her. He remembered how worried she was when Uncle Dan was missing. She wouldn't do this—not just because she was jealous. Not for any reason.

"I'm sure," he said finally. "Isabelle isn't the one messing up the program. You are Tempest St. Cloud. Or would you rather I called you Storm?"

"What are you talking about?" the woman shouted. "You think I did all this stuff to myself? Do I look crazy?"

Carter looked at her filthy, tattered dress, her tangled nest of hair, and the long sharp knife in her hand. She definitely did look crazy. Without another word, he turned and ran for the door.

"Carter, wait!"

He jerked the door open and ran into the darkness. He ran through the piles of limestone blocks and the fire pits, now barely glowing with coals. He heard Miss St. Cloud shouting his name, but her voice grew more distant as he ran until he couldn't hear her at all. Eventually, the sharp smell of the fires faded as well.

Finally, Carter stumbled to a stop near a gnarled tree. He leaned against it, huffing and panting. He was starting to feel dizzy and shaky. He'd been doing too much running. He was unsure how long he'd been in the suit. He needed out soon.

He looked around. Somehow he'd run completely out of the marsh and back into the graveyard. Gravestones rose up around him like a particularly grisly crop. He didn't remember seeing the cemetery wall, so the program was playing tricks on him again.

Then he froze. He heard Miss St. Cloud calling to him again. Her voice sounded far off but was clear. "You can't believe I'm behind this!" she shouted.

Carter slowly eased around the tree trunk until he was sure it was between him and Miss St. Cloud. He leaned against the rough bark and focused on breathing silently.

"Those hands in the graveyard," she called. "Remember how they half pulled my hair out? You can't think I wanted that to happen."

Carter remembered the fear on her face as the hands had seemed to be trying to pull her right through the dirt into the grave. Could she have been acting?

"Carter, why do you doubt me now?" Miss St. Cloud called.

Carter stepped out from around the tree to face Miss St. Cloud. She was still well out of reach and he already knew he could outrun her. "Isabelle told me you're Storm."

"And what did your uncle say?" she asked, putting her hands on her hips. "Surely Daniel doesn't go along with the absurd idea that I'm a hacker."

"I didn't talk to Uncle Dan," Carter admitted. "He was next door calling the police."

"Oh, he doesn't have a phone?" she asked dryly. "You have to see what's going on. Your cousin managed to contact you without Daniel hearing her. She's made this up to split us up."

Carter shook his head. "Isabelle might rain on me. She might even scare me half to death with zombie hands, but she wouldn't let someone attack me with a knife. We're family."

Even as he spoke, doubt crept in. He hadn't heard from Uncle Dan. And Isabelle hadn't answered when he'd called her. What if Miss St. Cloud was telling the truth? What if his own cousin would let him get hurt just so she could get back at Miss St. Cloud? Isabelle could be hot-tempered.

Carter shook his head again, this time to shake such thoughts out of it. He couldn't really believe his own cousin was doing this.

"Come on, Carter," Miss St. Cloud said.

"We've suffered all this together. Remember that rain?" she called. "I almost froze to death, too. Would I have done that if I was in control?"

Carter remembered the freezing rain and the feel of his teeth chattering. It had even made it hard to talk. His eyes narrowed as he thought about it. He didn't remember Miss St. Cloud having any trouble talking. Her teeth hadn't chattered. She hadn't gasped as she spoke. She hadn't acted cold.

How hard would it be for a master hacker to make her VR self look cold, wet, and miserable without actually feeling it? Somehow, Carter suspected it wouldn't be that difficult at all.

He began to back away from Miss St. Cloud. "I don't believe you. So just stay away from me."

Miss St. Cloud made a rude noise and began to stride across the graveyard toward him. With a groan, Carter spun around to run. How much more running could he survive?

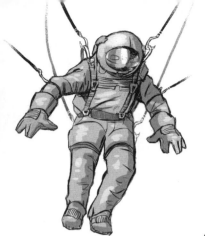

THE RIGHT TO REMAIN SILENT

Carter had barely gone two steps when a door appeared right between two gravestones in the middle of the cemetery. The door looked exactly like the door to Carter's bedroom, right down to the torn corner on the skateboarding poster taped to the center. Storm couldn't know what Carter's bedroom door looked like. Only family could know that.

He turned to look back at Miss St. Cloud. "It's time for me to go," he said. "It looks like Isabelle came through."

"Carter, don't go through there," she begged, still walking toward him. "Your cousin is just trying to split us up. She'll send you off into some side pocket of the program to cool your heels while she unleashes more zombies and iron bar killers on me. She won't have to pull any punches with you safe."

"I don't believe you."

"It makes sense," she said, taking a step toward him. "You're right. Your cousin doesn't want to hurt you. That's why we haven't suffered anything really dangerous. She didn't want to risk you."

Carter crossed his arms and shook his head. "I'm not buying it."

"Please, don't leave me in here alone."

Carter was shocked to see tears running down Miss St. Cloud's cheeks. She really looked scared. "Don't let her hurt me any more," the woman begged.

Carter looked at the glowing door and back at Miss St. Cloud. Was Storm just a fantastic actor, or had Carter's cousin really gone off the deep end? Who should he trust?

"Carter," Izzy's voice sounded in his ear, thin and panicky, "you've got to come through the door. I don't know how long I can keep it in place."

He decided. He spun and ran for the light. Suddenly, Orlick stepped from behind the glowing door. Blood soaked his coat. Carter felt his stomach lurch as he realized the man's skull was partially caved in. The smashed skull didn't seem to bother Orlick much. He lunged at Carter, swinging a knife that could double as a sword. Carter jumped up on top of the nearest tombstone. The knife blade sparked as it hit the stone and glanced off.

Carter jumped down and dodged around the staggering blacksmith. The blade whistled through the air, nicking off a swatch of Carter's jacket. Carter circled and ran back for the door. Just in front of it, writhing white hands burst through the soil. On some, the skin was split and wriggling things fell out. On others, bones alone shone in the moonlight. They all reached toward Carter as he ran.

Then something grabbed Carter from behind

102

and jerked him off his feet. He lay on his back looking up at Orlick. The bleeding man laughed. He raised his knife just as Carter kicked up, hard. His boot slammed into Orlick's knee with a sound that made Carter's stomach roll again.

Carter twisted out of the way as Orlick fell forward. Zombie hands caught at Orlick's head, pulling out handfuls of bloody hair. Gritting his teeth, Carter used Orlick like a bridge, stepping on the middle of the man's back to springboard over the zombie hands.

Finally with his hands on the doorknob, he heard one last call. "Carter, stop!"

He turned to see Miss St. Cloud running toward him. He turned the knob and leaped through the door and into total darkness.

This time the total darkness was the close, sweaty feel of the virtual reality suit. He had made it out. "Get me out of here!" he yelled.

"Just stay calm," Uncle Dan's voice spoke quietly in his ear. "Isabelle is coming."

Carter fought the urge to thrash around.

He'd never wanted out of the suit more than he did right that second. He nearly fell out the back when Isabelle opened the suit. The light of the suit room was the most wonderful thing he'd ever seen.

With a whoop of joy, Carter threw his arms around Isabelle and hugged her.

"Oh, gross," she complained as she pushed him away. "You're all wet and you smell bad!"

Carter just laughed. Then he headed out of the room. His legs felt a little wobbly and he barely got through the door into the computer lab when a wave of dizziness passed over him.

"Whoa," his uncle said and Carter felt his uncle's strong hand under his arm. "Come on over here and sit down."

Carter sat and Isabelle shoved a juice box into his hand. "Drink this," she said. "It should help."

Carter nodded, sucking up the juice eagerly. It tasted wonderful. He looked around and saw two police officers standing beside one of the computer monitors. Uncle Dan strode over to begin typing on a keyboard next to them.

Isabelle had left Carter's side and was walking around the room, flipping on small LED lanterns and smacking tap lights his uncle had stuck to the walls. Carter had never really noticed them before. The room already had plenty of light from the florescent fixtures that covered much of the ceiling.

"Okay, I'm ready," Uncle Dan said, looking up at the officers. "When I kill the power, the program will have to shut down. Isabelle will open the suit and you two should be able to arrest her without any kind of resistance."

"This is going down as my strangest arrest," one of the officers said as he strode toward the suit room. He was a younger man with rust-colored hair.

His partner was an older woman with a cheerful face who nearly had to skip to keep up with his long-legged stride. She didn't seem to mind though.

"Okay, I'm shutting down," Uncle Dan said. "In 3, 2, 1. Shutting down."

The lights went out all over the room and the continual soft hum of the computers fell silent. Carter hadn't even noticed the sound when the computers were on, but with them off the silence seemed loud.

Carter stood, ignoring a wave of dizziness and exhaustion. He walked shakily to the suit room door. Inside, Isabelle was just releasing the seal on the suit. Miss St. Cloud stepped backward onto the floor with far more grace than Carter had shown.

She snapped her head to glare at Isabelle. "You are a most annoying child," she said.

Just then, the tall officer pulled the hacker's wrists around behind her back and snapped on handcuffs.

"You have the right to remain silent," the other officer said, her voice still cheerful. "You have the right to an attorney."

Another wave of dizziness passed over

106

Carter, and he backed up carefully to his chair. On a table nearby were several more juice boxes. He tore the top off another one so he could pour the juice down in gulps instead of dainty sips. After one more, the dizziness passed.

The officers walked out of the suit room with Miss St. Cloud between them. She turned to smile at Carter, and he felt a chill. "That was such fun," she said. "We really will have to play again some time."

"Oh?" Isabelle's voice sounded from behind them. "Do they let prisoners do a lot of computer hacking?"

The cold eyes of the hacker turned back to Isabelle again. "I really don't like you."

Isabelle just smirked. "That just makes my day."

The officers pulled Miss St. Cloud, and she came along toward the door to the upstairs. Uncle Dan stood leaning in the doorway.

"You're lucky you didn't hurt my nephew,"

he said.

"You're just mad because you were foolish enough to believe me," she said.

He shrugged. "Luckily I had backup who saw right through you."

"This time."

Carter stood and took a step toward her. "Why did you let the zombie hands pull your hair? They were disgusting."

The hacker shrugged. "I fell. But you're right, they were disgusting. And my little accident almost convinced you I was innocent, didn't it?"

Carter shook his head. "Not really. The only way for you to be innocent was for Isabelle to be guilty and I knew she wasn't."

"So you say," the hacker said. "Now."

"Really, honey," the police officer said. "You have the right to remain silent. Why don't you go with that?"

Storm glared down at the slightly shorter officer, but she didn't bother to speak and soon they were out the door. Uncle Dan looked over at Carter. "How are you feeling?"

"Better now," Carter said. "You know, next time I could use a little faster rescue."

"It took us over an hour to even know you were in trouble," Uncle Dan said, shaking his head. "The virus Storm dumped in the system fed us messages and we believed they really were from you."

"We figure she got the snippets of your voice from the times we've played her game in the past," Isabelle said.

"So how did you figure out something was wrong?" Carter asked as he ran a hand through his sweaty hair.

"Your conversation was a little too weird," Isabelle said. "Even for you. Then we started asking questions and your answers didn't make sense at all."

Uncle Dan nodded. "When I poked around in the system, I discovered I was shut out of everything. Since the only way I could be hacked is by someone on the property, that meant the lovely Miss St. Cloud was a hacker."

"Well, she's off to jail," Isabelle said. "So we don't have to worry about her anymore."

Carter nodded, though he didn't feel as sure as Isabelle sounded. The hacker didn't act very defeated when the police arrested her. He had a sick feeling they hadn't seen the last of her.

With a shudder, he picked up another carton of juice. "Say, I'm starting to think I deserve hazardous duty pay."

Uncle Dan laughed. "How about your normal pay plus a pizza?"

"With anchovies?" Carter loved anchovies.

"That's disgusting," Isabelle said. "No stinky fish."

"Hey, I'm the one who had to fight zombies," Carter insisted. "I should get stinky fish if I want them."

"You already smell like a stinky fish," Isabelle said.

"Okay, guys." Uncle Dan held up his hands. "Two pizzas, one with stinky fish and one without. You two have earned them. But, first, um, Carter?"

"Yeah?"

"Go take a shower."

Carter laughed, happy to oblige and very happy to be done with that adventure. "As long as there's pizza waiting for me when I come out."

Uncle Dan grabbed his car keys. "Isabelle and I will go get it right now. You go ahead and take your shower."

"And burn your clothes," Isabelle said.

"Complain, complain," Carter snapped as he stood up and dumped the pile of empty juice boxes into the trash. "Next time you can fight evil in the suit."

"You're on."

Storm has been caught! Now that the hacker is behind bars, work has continued on the virtual reality suits. It's time for the big reveal. Everything will go perfectly now . . . Or will it?

Follow the adventure in

Book 5
Big City Blues
Back to Wonderland